Who Says Woof?

John Butler

VIKING

For Emily Victoria

VIKING
Published by the Penguin Group
Penguin Putnam Books for Young Readers,
345 Hudson Street, New York, New York 10014, U.S.A.
Penguin Books Ltd, 80 Strand, London WC2R 0RL, England
Penguin Books Australia Ltd, 250 Camberwell Road, Camberwell, Victoria 3124, Australia
Penguin Books Canada Ltd, 10 Alcorn Avenue, Toronto, Ontario, Canada M4V 3B2
Penguin Books (N.Z.) Ltd, 182-190 Wairau Road, Auckland 10, New Zealand

Penguin Books Ltd, Registered Offices: Harmondsworth, Middlesex, England

First published in Great Britain in 2003 by Puffin Books.
This edition published in 2003 by Viking, a division of Penguin Putnam Books for Young Readers.

1 3 5 7 9 10 8 6 4 2

Copyright © John Butler, 2003
All rights reserved

Library of Congress Cataloging-in-Publication Data is available
ISBN 0-670-03655-2

Printed in China
Set in Countryhouse

Who says woof?

A dog
says
woof.

Who says moo?

A cow says

moo.

Who says **Oink?**

A pig says **Oink.**

Who says hee-haw?

A donkey says

hee-
haw.

Who says

cluck?

A chicken
says
cluck.

Who says **neigh?**

A horse says

neigh.

Who says

meow?

A cat says **meow.**

Who says
baa?

A sheep says baa.

Who says
Squeak?

A mouse says **Squeak.**

Who says

quack

quack

quack

quack

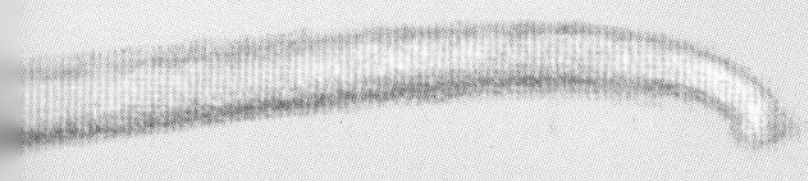

quack

quack?

A duck with lots
of ducklings says
quack

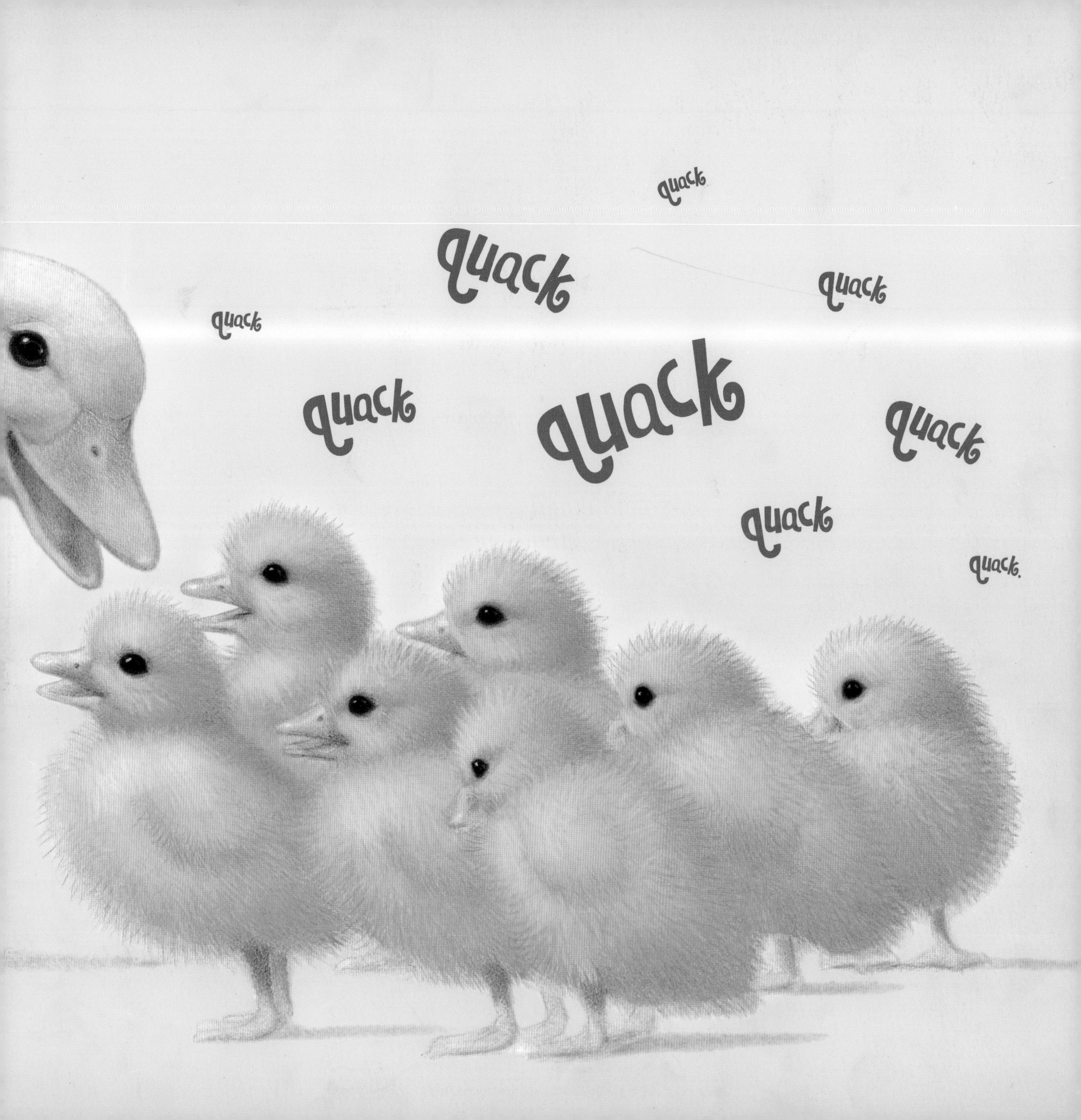
quack
quack
quack
quack
quack
quack
quack
quack
quack.

woof

moo

Oink

hee-haw

cluck

neigh

baa

meow

squeak

quack